The Great Race

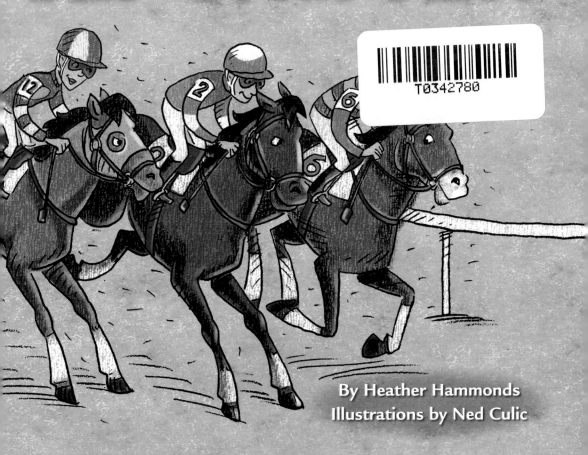

By Heather Hammonds
Illustrations by Ned Culic

Contents

Title	Text Type	Pages
The Great Race	*Narrative*	2–9
A Day at the Races	*Response*	10–16

The Great Race

The sun shone on the racetrack,
On the horses, strong and proud,
On the jockeys with their coloured shirts,
And the huge, excited crowd.

The horses were led to the start,
With their jockeys riding high,
And all the people waited,
To see their favourites fly.

3

The race began and the horses ran,
To the cheering of the crowd,
The race-caller yelled into his mic.
Oh! The noise was very loud.

The horses galloped speedily,
Tails flying in the breeze,
And even the race's slowest horse,
Went 'round the track with ease.

Number Six was out in front,
As the horses took the bend,
But Number Two was close behind,
How would this great race end?

Number Two drew closer,
Soon it was neck and neck,
Number Twelve then made her move,
She'd beat the others yet!

Down the final stretch they ran,
The crowd cheered and rose up.
"Go Six," they cried. "Go Two," they yelled.
"You'll win the Country Cup!"

But Number Six stretched forward,
To win the long, great race.
His jockey stood in victory,
A smile upon his face.

Subject: A Day at the Races

Dear Aunt Rebecca,

We went to watch some horse races today, at a racetrack out in the country.

We had lunch at the races and watched all the horses run.

It was an exciting day.

I thought the racetrack was very beautiful. It was covered in bright green grass with white rails on each side.

There were lots of brightly coloured flowers planted outside the rails and they had a sweet perfume.

The horses were tall and majestic. Their brown, black, grey and chestnut coloured coats shone in the sun. The jockeys who rode the horses wore silken shirts of different colours.

There were several races of different lengths during the day. Mum, Dad and I stood close to the fence and watched most of them.

At the start of each race, the horses galloped away together, in a long line. I liked the sound of their thundering hooves, as they pounded down the track.

The crowds watching the races cheered and shouted as their favourite horses ran. They made a lot of noise and I enjoyed cheering, too.

The horses stretched their necks forward and galloped as fast as they could to finish the race.

It was most exciting to see the winning horses cross the finish line.

After each race finished, the winning jockey got a shiny silver trophy and the horse got a light silk horse rug.

Wish you had been there!

Jane